Disney

Let's Go!

to the Dairy Farm

Random House New York

Published in the United States by Random House Children's Books, a division of Random House, Inc., New York, and simultaneously in Canada by Random House of Canada Limited, Toronto, in conjunction with Disney Enterprises, Inc. This work was originally published by Golden Books, an imprint of Random House Children's Books, a division of Random House, Inc., as three separate volumes: *Let's Go to the Dairy Farm*, published in 1998; *Let's Go to the Airport*, published in 1997; and *Let's Go to the Fire Station*, published in 1997.
RANDOM HOUSE and colophon are registered trademarks of Random House, Inc.

ISBN: 0-7364-2190-4
www.randomhouse.com/kids/disney
First Random House Edition
Printed in the United States of America
10 9 8 7 6 5 4 3 2 1

"Here we are at Grandma Duck's dairy farm," Donald said to his nephews Huey, Dewey, and Louie one summer morning. Mickey was with them, too. They had all promised to take care of Grandma's cows while she was on vacation.

"Grandma Duck left us lemonade—and plenty of instructions," said Mickey.

"Who needs instructions?" Donald replied. "I already know all about cows."

Mickey read Grandma's list. "It says here to milk the cows in the morning, put them out to pasture to eat grass, and then take them to the barn for their evening milking."

"I knew that," Donald said. Whistling a cheerful tune, he headed for the pasture. Mickey followed with Huey, Dewey, and Louie.

Mickey and the boys found the cows drinking from the farm pond. Mickey gave the largest one a gentle pat to get her started toward the barn. The other cows followed.

Donald saw one last cow standing behind a big, round bale of hay. “Here, cow, here, cow!” he called. But the cow wouldn’t come.

“I said, ‘Here, cow!’” Donald yelled, stomping toward the big animal.

Mickey, Huey, Dewey, and Louie hurried over to see what was happening. There, next to the big cow, stood a little calf.

“Why, this must be Rosie and her new calf!” Mickey exclaimed. “Grandma mentioned them specially in her instructions.”

"Grandma says to take Rosie's calf to the barn and help it drink from a bottle," Mickey said.

Donald tried to lead the calf in the direction of the barn. But Rosie blocked his way.

“Come on . . . move, you silly cow!” Donald ordered, trying to push Rosie aside. Rosie refused to budge, so Donald pushed again.

That made Rosie mad. Bellowing angrily, she pushed him back. A second later she was chasing Donald around the pasture!

Meanwhile, Mickey and the nephews had led the little calf to the barn and fed it from the bottle. Then they put the calf in a straw-filled stall.

"When Donald gets Rosie into the barn, we'll milk her. Then she can snuggle with her calf," Mickey told the boys.

Just then, Donald dashed into the barn with Rosie close behind him. He raced into a milking stall with Rosie right on his heels. Donald slipped away from the big cow, slammed the stall door shut, and leaned against it.

"Guess I showed *her* who's boss!" he said, wiping his forehead.

"You sure did!" Mickey agreed. He handed Donald a bucket of soapy water. "Now you can wash her before she's milked."

"Aw, phooey! Who ever heard of washing a cow?" Donald muttered. But he lugged the bucket into Rosie's stall.

Donald set the bucket down right behind Rosie.
Swish, swish! went Rosie's tail as she flicked it back and forth.
Plop! went the tail as she dipped it into the soapy water.
And *whap!* went the tail as Rosie smacked suds right in Donald's face!

Sputtering and muttering, Donald finally managed to get Rosie washed. He watched Mickey and the boys hook the other cows up to the milking machines.

“Now, *that* looks easy,” he said. But when he tried it with Rosie, she pushed him over and started to run.

“Whoa!” Donald shouted, grabbing her by the tail.

"Watch out, Unca Donald!" Huey shouted as Rosie dragged Donald through the barn. Donald's feet got tangled in the hoses that carried the milk to the storage tank.

Snap! One of the hoses came loose. Milk sprayed everywhere, soaking Donald from head to toe and splashing in his eyes.

With milk in his eyes, Donald couldn't see a thing. He stumbled over hoses, boots, and milk cans and bumped into doors. Finally he put his foot straight into a bucket, tripped, and fell into a feed bin.

“Oof!” Donald gasped as he climbed out covered with bits of mashed grain. “Yuck!” He pulled pieces of wheat stalks out of his sleeves.

While Donald dripped and fumed, Mickey helped Huey, Dewey, and Louie catch Rosie. They tied her up and began to clean the barn.

But Donald wasn't about to quit yet. He grabbed an old milking stool and a bucket and marched toward Rosie.

"I'm going to milk this cow the old-fashioned way—by hand!" he declared.

When Rosie saw Donald approaching, a sly glint came into her big brown eyes. As soon as he got close enough, she gave a powerful kick—*thunk!*—and sent him flying through the air.

Donald landed—*splash!*—headfirst in a full milk can!

Mickey pulled Donald out of the can. "You've helped enough for today," he said, trying not to smile. "We'll finish milking Rosie."

Rosie behaved herself perfectly while Mickey milked her and then when Huey, Dewey, and Louie put her in the box stall with her calf.

After their chores were finished, the gang trooped back to the house and sat down for a rest on the front porch.

Just then, Grandma Duck drove up. “I missed my cows too much to go on vacation,” she explained.

“Hmph! I hope I never see another cow again as long as I live!” Donald said grumpily.

“That’s too bad,” Grandma said. “Look what I brought you.”

She handed each one a box. When they saw what was inside, everyone began to laugh—even Donald. For in each box was a huge piece of milk chocolate, shaped just like a cow!

Disney

Let's Go!
to the Airport

"Wow! We're finally going on vacation," Mickey said to Minnie and Goofy as they arrived at the airport.

"Hawaii—here we come!" Minnie said happily.

"This is my very first airplane ride!" exclaimed Goofy excitedly. "Look, you guys," he said. "I even got a pilot's hat for the trip!"

TICKETS

At the check-in counter, the agent stamped Mickey's ticket and then Minnie's.

Goofy looked and looked for his, and finally found it stuck between two ham sandwiches he had packed for a snack.

The ticket agent stamped the ticket. "Now, don't lose this," she warned Goofy.

CHECK-IN

Goofy thought hard. “I know!” he exclaimed. “I’ll put it inside my pilot’s hat. That’s really safe.”

He tucked the ticket snugly inside the hat.

Just then, as a group of pilots hurried into the airline terminal, a stiff breeze blew Goofy's hat right off his head—*whoosh!*

"Stop that hat!" Goofy yelled, racing after it.

As Goofy chased his runaway hat, he bumped into the pilots, knocking their hats and flight bags in every direction.

"Gawrsh! I'm sorry!" Goofy apologized as he helped everyone pick up their belongings.

The pilots smiled, placed their hats back on their heads, and hurried off to their planes.

Goofy picked up the last hat and looked inside. “Oh, no!” he cried. “One of those pilots took my hat by mistake! And my ticket’s in it!”

“Don’t worry, Goofy,” said Mickey. “We’ll help you find the pilot who has your hat.”

X-RAY

Minnie put her bags through the X-ray machine and hurried down a long hall to the boarding area. She saw hundreds of people getting on and off planes, but she didn't see a single pilot anywhere.

Mickey knocked on the door of the air traffic control tower. Inside, people with radios were telling the pilots when to take off and land their planes.

"Could you please use your radios to ask the pilots if one of them has Goofy's hat and ticket?" Mickey asked.

Meanwhile, Goofy spotted a pilot walking toward the baggage claim area. Goofy ran after the pilot, but he tripped and fell—*klunk*—onto a baggage conveyor loaded with suitcases.

Around and around Goofy whirled until his head was spinning!

BAGGAGE
CLAIM

Goofy staggered off the conveyor and stumbled through a door that led to the edge of the airfield. A plane was taxiing past slowly.

Through the cockpit window, Goofy saw a pilot wearing a hat that looked like his.

"Stop! Stop!" Goofy shouted, waving his arms.

In the control tower, the air traffic controllers saw Goofy waving his arms.

"Goofy is signaling us to stop that plane," one of the controllers said.

She radioed the pilot who was flying the plane. Quickly, the startled pilot stepped on the brakes.

Then Goofy saw another plane going by, and another, and another. All the pilots were wearing hats like his!

"Stop! Stop!" Goofy shouted, waving his arms again.

The traffic controllers radioed all the pilots to stop their planes. Soon Goofy had brought the whole airport to a standstill.

Suddenly one of the pilots began waving at Goofy.

"I heard the control tower's announcement," the pilot shouted. "I've got your hat! Come and get it!"

Goofy ran up to the door of the plane, and the pilot handed him his hat. Luckily, the ticket was still tucked safely inside!

Finally, it was time for Mickey, Minnie, and Goofy to board their plane. The flight attendant tore off part of Goofy's ticket and handed the rest back to him.

"That's your return ticket," Mickey explained to Goofy as they sat down and buckled their seat belts. "If you lose it, you won't be able to fly home."

"Don't worry," Goofy said. "This time I'm putting it in a really safe place—my shoe!"

Disney

Let's Go!

to the Fire Station

"Let's paint racing stripes on the old engine!" Huey exclaimed.

Mickey Mouse laughed. "Hold it!" he said. "We still want it to look like a fire truck." Mickey and the boys were on their way to the fire station. They had offered to decorate an antique fire engine for the Town Day parade the next day.

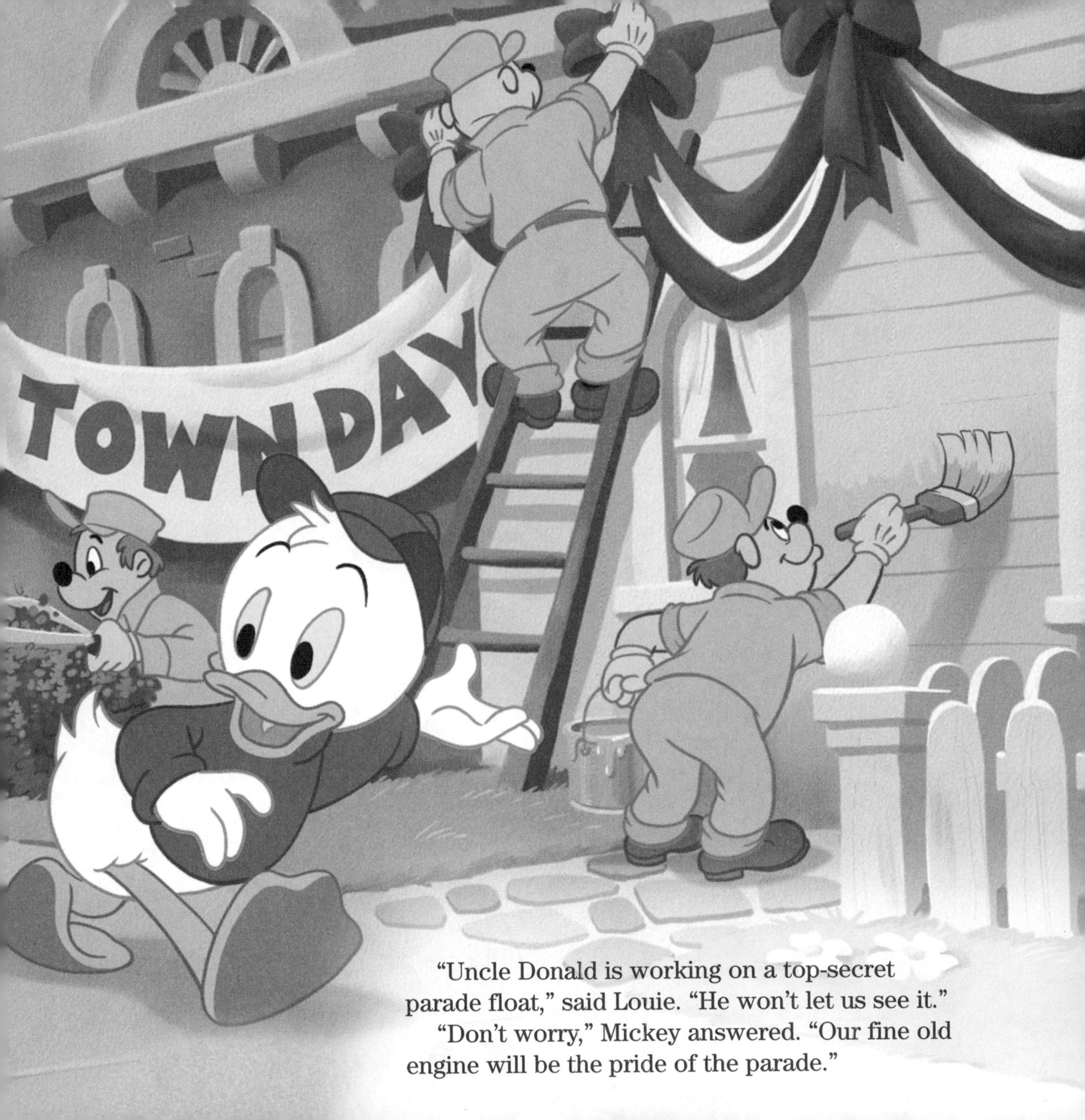

“Uncle Donald is working on a top-secret parade float,” said Louie. “He won’t let us see it.”

“Don’t worry,” Mickey answered. “Our fine old engine will be the pride of the parade.”

Mickey and the others arrived just in time to see their friend Goofy slide down the brass pole in the middle of the fire station.

"Hiya, gang," said Goofy.

"Goofy is a junior volunteer, just like me," Mickey told the boys as he leaned over to pat a friendly Dalmatian. "This is Freckles, the fire station's mascot."

"Here's our parade engine." Goofy grinned as he led the boys to an old-fashioned pumper truck. "Isn't she a beauty?"

Mickey started polishing the engine while Goofy and the boys went to work on the decorations.

“Does this truck still work?” asked one of the boys.

Mickey nodded. “Yes, it works, but it’s not as fast or as powerful as the newer engines. Now we just use it for parades.”

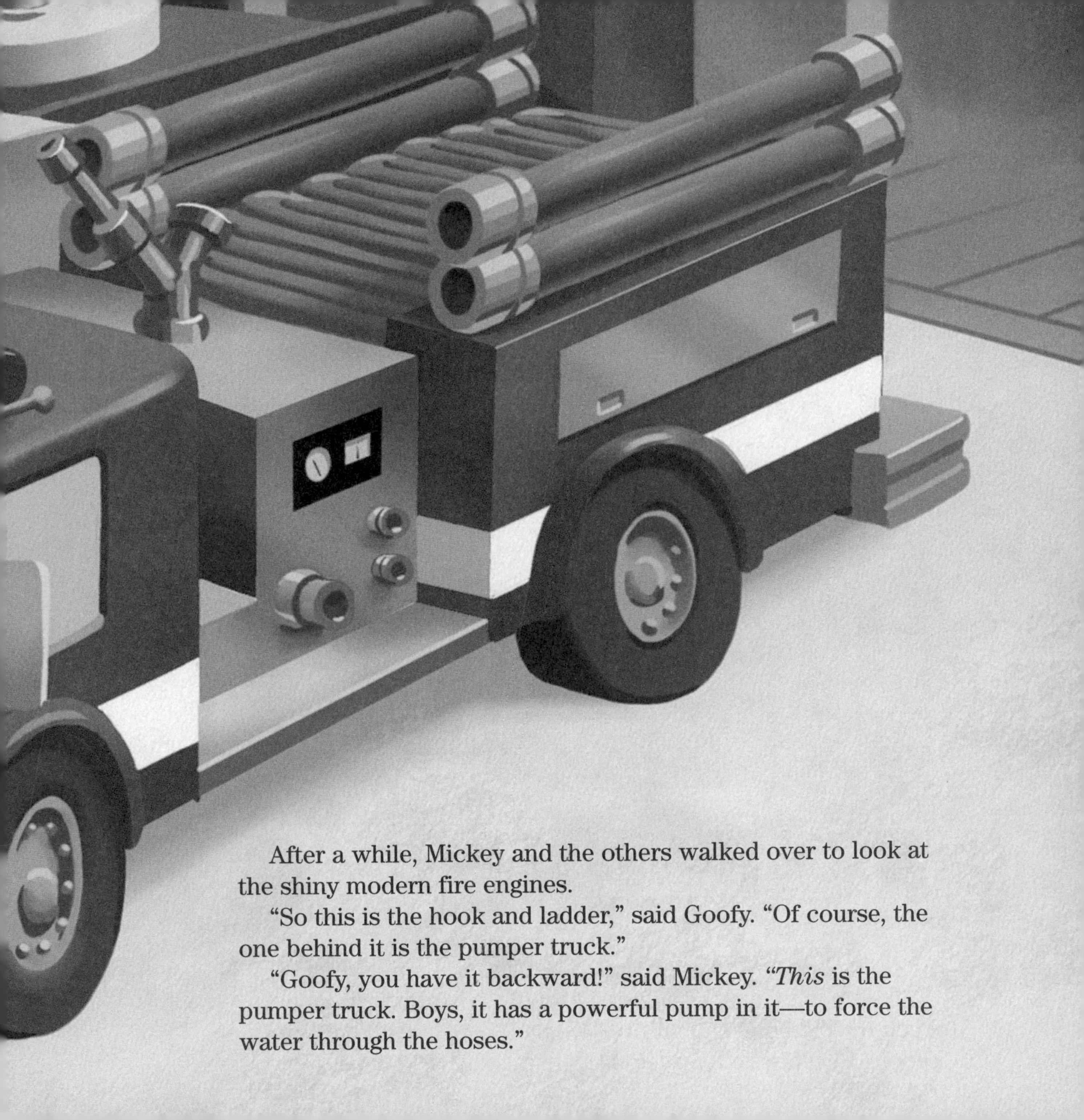

After a while, Mickey and the others walked over to look at the shiny modern fire engines.

"So this is the hook and ladder," said Goofy. "Of course, the one behind it is the pumper truck."

"Goofy, you have it backward!" said Mickey. "*This* is the pumper truck. Boys, it has a powerful pump in it—to force the water through the hoses."

“It must be hard work being a firefighter,” Louie said.

“It sure is,” Goofy responded proudly. “Do you remember when the big hotel caught fire? We had to rescue about twenty people. I even saved Mrs. Porter’s parakeet.”

“Gosh, Goofy,” said Mickey. “If I remember right, the regular firefighters rescued the parakeet. They just gave it to you to hold.”

“But I was a big help,” Goofy insisted. “I went and found Mrs. Porter and gave her back her bird.”

Then Goofy changed the subject.

"I'll tell you another story, boys," he said. "A couple of years ago, there was a big fire in the park outside town."

"What happened?" the boys asked eagerly.

"A campfire roared out of control," said Goofy. "But I rushed boldly into the forest. That night we saved the woods from being burned to the ground."

“I remember that night,” said Mickey. “It was cold. You and I passed blankets out to the campers. I don’t remember doing much else.”

Goofy looked embarrassed. After that, he didn't tell any more stories. He and the others finally finished decorating the engine and headed home together. Everybody looked forward to the next day—the day of the big parade.

The following day, the whole town turned out to watch the parade. The antique truck led the way—with Mickey at the wheel. The boys were allowed to ride in the back with Goofy.

"We're going to win the blue ribbon for best parade entry," said Huey. He looked back over his shoulder. "Uncle Donald's float doesn't have a chance."

TOWN DAY

Donald's float was just behind the fire engine. He had mounted a spaceship on his old pickup truck.

“Hey, Donald!” someone called from the crowd. “Is that a real rocket ship?”

“Almost,” Donald answered proudly. “Get a good look. My float is going to send the judges to the moon.”

Donald drove his wobbly rocket on down the street, sparks flying everywhere.

Suddenly, the rocket caught fire. Within seconds, the whole float was in flames.

"Help!" squawked Donald. "Fire!"

"I'll save you!" Goofy cried. As Mickey pulled to a stop, Goofy jumped off the fire truck. He grabbed one of the old engine's hoses and hooked it to a nearby hydrant. Then Goofy began spraying Donald's float with water. Before long, the fire was completely out.

Goofy was a hero at last. During the award ceremony after the parade, the mayor asked him to come forward.

"Goofy, I'd like you to accept this blue ribbon with our thanks," said the mayor. "You were very brave today. In fact, you're the bravest junior volunteer who ever held a hose!"